Two feet.

Two feet in blue socks.

Two feet in blue socks
in yellow boots.

Two feet in blue socks
in yellow boots walking.

Two feet in blue socks
in yellow boots walking in a puddle.

That feels good!

Two feet in blue socks in yellow boots walking in a muddy puddle.

Two feet in blue socks in yellow boots walking in a deep muddy puddle.

Two feet in blue socks
in yellow boots walking
in a very deep muddy puddle.

That feels good!

Two feet in blue socks in yellow boots

walking in a very, very deep . . .   Yuk!

Two cold, wet, muddy feet
in cold, wet, muddy, blue socks
in cold, wet, muddy, yellow boots
in a very, very deep, muddy puddle.

That doesn't feel good!

Two feet.